Hans Starrholm's mother fails to come home on the night the wall is erected across Berlin. Hans lives in West Berlin, but his mother had taken fresh vegetables to Cousin Hannah in East Berlin, as she had done many other days.

Hans succeeds in crossing the wall and makes his way to Cousin Hannah's home. In the course of the night and following morning, he learns for the first time of how his father died and the true reason for his mother's visits to the other side of Berlin. At fourteen, Hans grows out of boyhood during the *Night of the Wall.*

PRISCILLA GOLDTHWAIT was sent to Germany after World War II to set up a displaced persons camp for Russian refugees, operated by the United Nations Relief and Rehabilitation Association. When she returned to the United States, she spoke wherever possible about refugee and immigration problems. She later returned to Europe and met the "real Hannah" who inspired her to write *Night of the Wall.* Mrs. Goldthwait visited the infamous wall in August of 1963. This is her first book.

NIGHT OF THE WALL

Hans Starrholm's mother fails to come home the night the infamous wall is erected across Berlin. Hans lives in West Berlin, but his mother had frequently taken fresh vegetables to Cousin Hannah in East Berlin. Hans succeeds in crossing the wall and makes his way to his cousin's home. In the course of the night and the following morning, he learns for the first time how his father died and the secret reason for his mother's visits to Cousin Hannah. At fourteen, he grows out of boyhood during the *Night of the Wall*.

NIGHT OF THE WALL

by PRISCILLA GOLDTHWAIT

illustrated by DENNY McMAINS

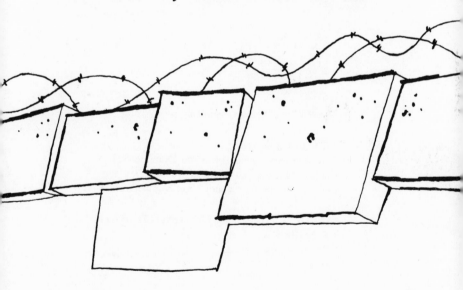

G. P. PUTNAM'S SONS   NEW YORK

To the real Hannah in Berlin

NIGHT OF THE WALL

Is it True?

The world is divided today in many places, usually by an invisible line.

In Berlin, that line is a visible stone wall which parts families from each other and tries to separate their loyalties. This is a story of such a family.

My children ask me if this story is true. I should say yes and no: the characters in *Night of the Wall* are fictional. But I am thinking of people I know.

Some of the incidents actually happened.

I have changed the geography and names and descriptions of places because *Night of the Wall* is not meant to be true in detail. It is meant to be true in spirit, true to the daring of many people who have helped others, or who have been caught themselves behind a wall and refused to give up.

I

THUNDER rumbled somewhere in the distance, but Hans Starrholm didn't hear it. The rain tapped on the window but he slept on. His head lay back on the couch; his bony knees sprawled out in front of him. It had been a long day of cycling and he was tired.

Slowly the dark of that August evening crept through the house. The clock ticked on the mantle. From the kitchen window, lightning played over two white plates and the untouched silver on the table.

Another noise of thunder—closer this time. Hans woke with a start.

7

"Mother?" he called, staring about him. How had it gotten so dark? He must have slept a long time.

The lightning flashed through the lace curtains. Looking out, he saw the purple sky above ink-black roofs. The wet street was empty.

He switched on the lamp, looking at the hook by the front door. But his mother's coat was not there. The clock on the mantle said 10:20; its tick was like snapping fingers.

Was it the storm that kept her so long? She had never been this late when she crossed to the other side.

These weekly trips over the boundary were not necessary! It made him angry every time he thought about Cousin Hannah. Of course she was sick a lot and food was short. But still! Hannah knew the trouble his mother went to every week, dragging a cart of vegetables and fruit all the way over there. All that food was a sacrifice, too; their tiny garden hardly grew enough to feed his mother, himself and Aunt Grace. Not to mention the medicine and vitamins and heaven knows what more his mother brought from her pharmacy without charging for them.

8

The pharmacy! Perhaps she was there. Crossing the living room, he opened the door. The lamp made a pool of light beside the cash register.

"Mutti?" he called eagerly. Then he saw a note on the counter.

HANS,
>   Have gone as usual to Hannah's.
>   Sorry to miss you. Will be back by supper-time.
>
>   Love, MUTTI.

Then she had expected to be back before now! Guiltily, he wondered what she meant by "Sorry to miss you." Would she have let him go with her if he had come home on time? But he had forgotten she was going today. And long ago he had given up asking if he could go with her. He couldn't bear to see that expression on her face. The closed look that told him the subject was not for discussion.

"But, Mutti, I'm almost fourteen," he'd say.

Instead of laughing, she'd crinkle her eyes and pat his shoulder. "Oh, oh, don't I know it!" But then she'd look past him, and he knew she was thinking of other times and of his dead father. "Time enough—time enough," she'd say.

And it was no use to ask, "But couldn't I just push the cart for you?"

Stooping, he saw his face in the back of the chrome cash register. His sunburned nose looked squashed in the crooked mirror. He stood up, impatiently slicking down the shock of brown hair. He couldn't help it if he looked boyish; he *was* almost fourteen.

Another sound like thunder brought him to the front window. But the sky was a clear night blue. Was that sound thunder? It was more like heavy objects bumping together. Sniffing something good, he went to the kitchen. He filled his bowl from a pot on the stove and ate hungrily. He felt better then, telling himself that his mother was all right. She had been making this trip alone for as long as he could remember.

Just the same, he thought, eating some bread, the trip is harder now. Instead of just walking across the boundary check point as she used to do, she had to have a permit. And there were soldiers with guns. Certain things were no longer allowed to be carried to the other side, and so the baggage inspection was strict. Only last week the guards had brought her into the guardhouse to search through her pockets. It made him furious, remembering this. No wonder she was more tired, more silent each time she returned from these visits. Perfectly ridiculous, anyway! Trying to divide a whole city into two halves. Trying to control the comings and goings across the boundary with permission cards and armed soldiers.

He remembered what it was like the last time he'd gone over. Soldiers in black uniforms. Loudspeakers on the streets telling people what to do. Nothing pretty in the stores. Lines of people waiting for potatoes. No one chatting or waving from a doorway. Not even kids playing ball any more.

Why should his mother bother going over there! Hannah had another aunt who took care of her. And anyway, Hannah wasn't a very close relative; their fathers had been distant cousins. He sighed, not wanting to remember.

Eight years ago his own father had died suddenly. That same year Hannah's father got into some kind of trouble, was taken away by the police, and sent to prison. Why should his mother be so generous to people like that? But she told Hans she felt sorry for the child's not having anyone "close to her." Child! She was a year older than he was.

12

Suddenly headlights flashed through the front window. A car drove by too fast, straining its motor. Setting the bowl down, he hurried to the living room. Several dark figures carrying suitcases and bundles trotted by in the street, looking over their shoulders.

The street lamps came on like pink blossoms through a mist rising from the wet stones. Then he heard the *clop clop* of a woman's shoes. Someone was coming, head and shoulders wrapped in a shawl. Her feet were hidden by the mist; she seemed to float toward him. She carried a big sack like his mother's.

"Mother?" Hans rapped on the window. The woman looked up. Hans gasped at the stranger's face—so pulled in at the mouth and dark under her eyes. She seemed to shrink from him and hurried on.

What's the matter with her? She seemed so— frightened.

He opened the door and looked down the street after her. She was almost running. The air felt clammy from the mist thinning away into the darkness. Again that droning rumble sounded from another direction, then the long roar ending with

13

the bumping thuds. Hans went out on the steps to look.

At the end of his street, he saw a crowd of people standing around a truck and a tall crane. Stones were being dumped from the back of the truck to the ground with that low, crackling sound like thunder.

What is this—road repairs this time of night? Curious, Hans took his jacket and walked out of the house and across the street toward the crane.

Suddenly two soldiers climbed up on something, holding their rifles horizontally above the heads of the crowd.

One of them shouted: "All right now. Break it up. Go back home and there won't be any trouble." His voice got loud. "It is forbidden to cross this barrier."

The crowd murmured, shuffling back as the soldiers climbed down. Elbowing closer, Hans suddenly saw that they were standing beside a wall of cement blocks that reached all across the end of his street. Stupefied, he watched the crane swing another stone into place beside the part of the wall already built. Two workmen quickly slapped cement around the edges with trowels.

14

A wall cutting off the end of his street so no one could come or go?

"What's happening? What is this wall for?" he asked a woman next to him.

"I don't know, I don't know—we can't go over there any more. We can't go over. And they can't come over here."

For minutes more the crowd watched, hypnotized as a new stone was laid, another cemented on top, and then another. Soon the whole street would be completely blocked off by a wall higher than his head.

Suddenly the people began pushing toward the last open space. They pushed Hans with them, jamming together across the last yard of street, up over the sidewalk against a house. As two soldiers quickly slung a rope across the opening, a sudden breath like a sigh passed from one person to another.

Over the rope, Hans faced a second muttering crowd. Several men shook their fists at the soldiers. Voices called: "What is this?" "Are we prisoners?"

A woman ducked under the rope, dragging a sack, and disappeared in back of Hans. One of the soldiers holding the rope shouted after her an-

15

grily. A girl with a suitcase slipped past the end of the wall. Hans stepped aside as the crowd made a path for her. She lost herself among them in the dark, but her red scarf fluttered down by the street lamp.

Another soldier chased after her, but the crowd blocked his way and he tripped on the curb. Getting up, he shook the scarf in his fist. Then he threw it down, and taking his gun, fired into the air.

The crowd on the other side was shocked to stillness. Then came a murmuring.

"He shouldn't—have done that," an old man stammered. The people beside him came to life. Some tried to shake their fists. Angry faces looked at one another. Others froze and moved away as more soldiers came up to the barrier.

The woman beside Hans began to cry. Hans tried to think what it all meant.

Was this wall going all across the city? Did it mean his mother could not get back over it? Where was she by now?

He watched the crane nose up onto the sidewalk. Only minutes ago the girl and the woman had run through here and escaped. Escaped! He

16

felt the skin prickle up his back. Does this wall mean that from now on people on the other side can only cross over by running past soldiers?

His legs began to tremble. Turning suddenly, he pushed his way back out of the crowd. He began to run. He'd have to find his mother. Perhaps if he kept going in the same direction as the wall, he'd find a way to get through. He must find a way to reach her and bring her home.

II

Hans stopped running. He was out of breath, and anyway, where did he want to go? Reaching an intersection, he again saw the wall to the left, another crane lifting and humming, the commotion of trucks. People stood along the sidewalk, on their front steps, at the street corners—motionless, quiet. A few whispered among themselves. One old man was crying, his face in his hands. Hans looked away, shocked to see a grownup cry.

Was his mother caught behind the wall? He could go to the bridge where she always crossed over and see if he could find her. He must make sure she was all right! Yes, he'd go there.

Again running parallel to the wall but a long block away, he turned right and then left several times until he could see the bridge ahead of him at the end of the street. A crowd had gathered under the street light by the sentry box. Hans walked toward it and saw the tall reeds on the riverbank off to the right. Had the wall really stopped at the river? But no, in the distance where the river left the main street, curving away to the country, he saw the shoulder of stone begin again.

He stopped at the edge of the restless crowd. Normally only a wobbly line of people, staring blankly, waited beside their bundles, to show their pass permits. But now the crowd strained against the pole barrier.

The old soldier had to raise his voice. "Come on, get back there. Hey! You can't come over now. You know that."

"Yes, we know," said someone.

"How about my husband? Can't he come back?" said another.

"Yes, and my daughter. She's over there. She has a permit."

"Sure, I know. Sure. And I hope you know it's not me doing this. I'm under orders." The soldier's voice got shrill and he patted his forehead with a red handkerchief. "You'll have news of your friends and relatives as soon as possible." He tried to speak calmly.

"What does that mean?" a man snarled. "You know they always say that over there when—"

"I already told you. Those what live over there have to stay. But the visitors will be allowed back —later."

"My mother should be coming back . . ." Hans looked past the soldier, at the empty bridge.

"But when, when?" said another.

"*Ach,* I already told you." The soldier pulled out his handkerchief again.

Suddenly the crowd was quiet. Hans couldn't see what had hushed them until he heard footsteps on the wooden planks. Pushing to the front, he saw an officer in black striding across the shadowed bridge into the lamplight.

Halting sharply, he glared at the little soldier, who hastily stuffed his handkerchief in his pocket and saluted. As the officer gave orders he talked at the crowd from the side of his mouth, not looking at them. "No persons will cross tonight in any direction with or without papers. All gatherings

21

will disband immediately—people should be off the streets at this hour." Answering the nervous salute of the soldier, he turned to go.

"But my mother?" Hans heard himself saying.

"No questions, boy," said the officer, glancing back again.

"But where is my mother?" Hans meant to add "sir," but he looked away from the glitter of the man's eyes under the lamplight.

"Never mind about your mother. Whatever the Leader does is for the good of the people."

"But why do you put people behind a wall, like —like prisoners?"

A murmur, some shushing, went through the crowd. Someone nudged Hans.

The officer pressed his lips together. "We will keep as many behind walls as necessary." He jerked his chin to emphasize the words, and his eyes kept moving over their faces. He pulled a paper from his breast pocket.

"What's your mother's name?"

"Starrholm, Maria." Hans' heart pounded. He should not have told him. Through the back of the page, under the lamp's ray, he could see a list of names.

The officer scanned the page. "Bringing food to a sick relative, eh?"

Hans nodded but his voice didn't make any sound.

"I hope for your mother's sake that she is telling the truth." The man folded the paper, replacing it. "Anyway, we're watching her. Starrholm, eh? It seems you have quite some black sheep for relatives!" He gave a hard little laugh, then turned and strode away, his footsteps echoing and re-echoing across the dark boards.

Hans didn't move except for his eyes. Peering toward the white pole barrier at the far end, he lost sight of the dark figure in the shadows of the night. He could feel the murmur, the movement in the crowd around him.

Someone patted his shoulder. A woman's voice said: "Maybe she'll come later."

Someone else whispered: "Poor boy." Several faces went wagging past him.

"That's what happened last month to Liza and they never saw her again."

Hans numbly walked away from the bridge. Making a path through the long grass, he climbed down the embankment.

"Come on, young fellow, you aren't allowed to go down there."

Hans sensed pity in the voice of the soldier calling from the rail of the bridge. Straining through the darkness, he tried to see a face on the other shore. But only a long line of reeds waved back at him from the empty riverbank. Tears pricked his eyes but he swallowed hard.

"We will keep as many behind walls as necessary." "Bringing food to a sick relative, eh?" ". . . hope she's telling the truth."

Telling the truth? Of course she was telling the truth. Why not?

But then the officer had said: "Anyway, we're watching her." ". . . some black sheep for relatives."

What did he mean?

"Say, son," the soldier called gently, "you'll have to be moving out of there or you'll be getting me into trouble."

Hans climbed up the bank and began to run on beside the river. He would have to get to his mother somehow and warn her. He should be thinking how to do it, but he couldn't seem to think. He just kept on running from the bridge and the

black-uniformed officer. The words: "Black sheep
. . . tell the truth . . . waiting for her . . . black
sheep . . . tell the truth . . . waiting for her . . ."
pounded in his head. At last he stopped to catch
his breath. Moonlight suddenly glinted over the
wet, black street, filling a puddle with silver. Over
his shoulder, he looked at the moon emerging from
the clouds. And he burst into a sob.

It's because of that wretched girl Hannah! It's
all her fault! And her father, he had trouble with
the police—a criminal maybe. That's what the
man meant by "black-sheep relatives."

But what had that to do with his mother? Why
should they blame her? What was the rest of the
truth? Breathing more quietly, he looked ahead at
the river. Now, only a block away, the stones began again. The cranes and trucks had done their
work and gone. But he saw the head of a mason
working with his trowel. A nearby sentry was talking to a friend, thumbs in his belt. Was it possible
to sneak through when the guards weren't looking?

A few last pedestrians with strained faces jogged
by him. He walked on. Block after block he jogged
alongside the barrier past the sentries and masons.
Once he saw a chance to cross: a soldier had left
his post by a gap between two stones, to talk to a

girl. And the guard on the other side was waving to someone behind him. Now Hans could run through. But in a moment both sentries had again turned around to the wall.

Sick at losing his chance, Hans kept on. Scared or not, he would have to get over. But how? And once over the wall, would he find his mother? She would have started home from Hannah's house hours ago, wouldn't she? Or was she already in trouble with the police?

A pebble scudded from one of his shoes as he found himself crossing a vacant lot. Beyond, the wall joined itself to the side of a ramshackle building. Broken windows were boarded up or crisscrossed with wire. Something silver glittered in a shadowed doorway. A sentry raised his canteen to take a drink. Hans quickly ran past him as the town clock tolled the hour. There was no one else on the street; he would have to stay out of sight.

Beyond the building was a high tangle of barbed-wire coils. Next, a double line of wooden posts strung with more wire continued across another back lot and along a dirt road. As Hans couldn't see more guards by the wall, he was sure the wire was electric, and dared not go near it.

Continuing along the wall, he saw that the posts

and wire stopped suddenly. Behind them, the road curved away to the left. And straight ahead, east, nothing—no wall of any kind! Instead, a moonlit meadow shaggy with grass and daisies and clumps of trees. And in the distance, a forest. That must be Mayerling Forest. He had reached the city limits!

Wind ruffled some trees beyond the barbed wire. The wet leaves fell on the road. He saw how the stones there had been ripped up and broken and thrown to the weeds. He looked away, with a lump in his throat.

Just then a dog barked. He was almost sure of it. The sound seemed to come from the nearest thicket. He'd better get out of sight before the soldier with the canteen saw him. Looking around, he walked to the edge of the grass. There's nothing to stop me from crossing here. He stared out over the endless sheen of meadow.

Once I step into that moonlight, I'll be like a black bug on a whitewashed wall. But if I could make that first bush. And then the thicket. And then—his breath skipped—"Mayerling Forest." For a minute he was sure he could do it. He could run from bush to tree until he reached the forest.

Then he could follow the regular path through the forest to the village and back to Hannah's house in the city, without any wall to stop him.

But would he dare? Alone in that darkness, the breathing sounds of the forest were like those of a huge animal lying in wait. He swallowed hard. He could never make it. He'd better go back.

Then he remembered the warning—to get off the streets. He couldn't go back now. A soldier might arrest him—maybe send him to jail. He dug his nails into his hands until they hurt, closing his eyes. It was decided for him. He'd have to go on.

Lowering his head, he dived into the moonlight, running for the bush as fast as he could.

III

THE grass was slippery. Hans didn't reach the bush as fast as he had hoped. As he tried to creep under it, he felt something pushing him back. He couldn't find a space to squeeze through; his heart began to pound. At last, by bending double, he managed to push through one wide triangle of space, but in his hurry, the barbed wire scratched down the front of his short pants, tearing the skin below his knee.

He thrashed his way into the thick, low branches, breaking them down to make a place for himself. Sinking on all fours, he stared out to see if someone had heard. His eyes were level with the tassels of grass.

31

Except for his own breath and the lisping of a breeze, he could hear nothing. A bird trilled once by the road and his heart stopped. But gradually, as nothing more was seen or heard, his breathing became more natural. His leg hurt, and he sat back to soak up the trickling blood with a handkerchief.

It was such a relief to feel safe that he thought of staying where he was, at least until morning. But then what would happen in daylight? All the easier for a border guard to spot him. If only he did not have to go through the dark forest. If he could just run across the meadow until he reached the highroad somewhere ahead in the distance. But the risk. Black bug on a whitewashed wall. Again he peered around him for some sign of life. Surely there would be a border patrol, or was this wire their barrier?

Suddenly from the Mayerling Forest a light beamed and went out. He watched, sitting up, hardly breathing. Yes, there it came on again—and went out. It seemed to pause and then come on. Was it a signal? The third time, squinting, he could see that during the pause the beam kept moving off to one side against a mass of trees. Then it disappeared. It was a revolving light. A searchlight from Mayerling Forest! His skin puckered under his damp shirt, and he realized how wet his pants were from sitting on the ground. He dried his palms on his hips and turned to look for his next objective. No sense to think of running for the highroad where the searchlight might spot him. His next stop would be behind the next thicket. Crouching, he began to run.

If I keep my head down and keep running low, perhaps I'll look like an animal, he told himself. But his heart throbbed as the moonlight poured over him again.

He reached the next glade and threw himself down behind two tree trunks. Staying long enough to catch his breath, he crept farther on his hands and knees, to find a pile of unclipped branches thrown across the path. Stumbling over it, unnerved by this second barrier, he burrowed into a thicket.

It was pitch black now, except for quivers of moonlight on the matted leaves and branches. With his hands before his face, Hans could barely move through the close growth. Underbrush held his feet; twigs and branches shook, drenching his shoulders with leftover rain. After a few moments, he knew he had lost all sense of direction and had no idea how far or which way he had come. He stopped, feeling almost drowned in the wet darkness. He wanted to scream with terror. Something furry brushed his leg. Two lights, like little marbles, stared at him from a tree. The hairs on the back of his neck began to tingle, and he loosened his shirt collar. Digging his fingernails into his palms, he kept on. He was lost—he was lost. For a little more he struggled on because he dared not stop. But when he reached a thick pine with wide branches, he grabbed onto the lowest one with relief. Hoisting himself up, he crouched on it to calm his heaving, trembling body.

The drips of rain from the branches felt good on his back. And the tiny sounds of the wet, breathing woods did not frighten him; occasional squeaks and scuttling sounds seemed a relief. Perhaps they covered what seemed to him the thunderous sounds of the branches. An owl went *ooh-ooh* overhead, and he almost ignored it. Slowly he began to climb higher, spurred by the thought that from higher up he could see where he was.

As he neared the treetop, a harsh undertone called: "Corporal, this way. I know I heard it. Bring Dart over here."

Hans froze to the limb. The voice sounded so near, almost under him but to the left. Very slowly, he moved his head around. At first he could see nothing but a lattice of branches against the grayish moonlight.

Then another voice came from another direction: "No, not that way."

Hans peered around the trunk of the tree. The second voice seemed to come from up in the air. A light caught the corner of his eye.

"Douse the light, will you?" the first voice said.

Waiting a moment, Hans very slowly inched out on his limb and parted the branches. He was looking over the edge of his thicket across a patch of field into the next tangle of trees. A flashlight shone from the window of a small tower there, like a box high up on four spindle legs with a strawlike roof. The light disappeared.

A soldier peered out through binoculars. "Where are you, anyway?" he called in a loud whisper.

Below Hans, another flashlight answered off to the right. A soldier stepped out of the bushes and beckoned to the one in the tower, who waved an answer and in a moment appeared in the clearing with a police dog. Straining at the leash, the dog pulled the soldier across the clearing almost beneath Hans' tree.

"See, I told you. Look how excited he is." With the dog sniffing the ground, they disappeared around the right side of the thicket, where Hans had entered it.

Hans knew he must move somehow. It wouldn't be long before the dog would follow his scent back into the bushes again. His heart was beating rapidly and he felt an iciness creeping through him. He tried to look out from his perch to locate the meadow and Mayerling Forest, but the branches were too heavy to separate. He began to crawl back along the branch to the trunk. Like someone in slow motion, he clambered down. Desperately, he looked from side to side for a space through which to see the soldiers or the meadow.

Halfway down he saw a triangle of light at the end of a thin branch. Crawling forward onto it, he gazed out on the silvery meadow. In the distance to the right was the black Mayerling Forest and its peering eye of light. The moon was overhead now. He felt dizzy with the shimmer of the light and sick from the pounding of his heart. No sound came from the soldiers, but Hans leaned out, looking back to the road and that first bush where he had hidden. The soldiers were there, walking from the meadow onto the road by the posts. And the dog was pulling on the leash, his nose to the ground. They had found his tracks all right, but the dog was following them backward! He felt a laugh inside but he couldn't make a sound.

Hans looked ahead at the meadow. He must get going. But it was so bright out there. He should run for the next thicket behind him, but that was where the soldiers had come from. Maybe there were more of them in those towers. Something again shimmered in his eyes until he had to squint. Then he opened them wider. The river! Of course. That dark, wide, flickering place across the meadow beyond the fringe of tall reeds was Mayerling River! As if from an electric shock, his thoughts cleared. If he could run at the right moment, he could take a short cut straight to the river and swim over it to Mayerling Village. No dog can smell tracks on water. No need to go through the forest. Hope wrenched with agony inside him —how sure his timing would have to be for this thicket of woods to act as a screen.

He leaned out again to look for the dog and the

soldiers. If he ran now—they were standing on the road looking in all directions—he would certainly be seen. But if he waited. His mind churned. If he waited until the right moment. Now he saw them turn around, the hound straining up on his hind legs, to go back to the meadow, ears sharp like a wild creature baying at the moon. If Hans could bring himself to wait until they were back near him, with the trees between him and them— and then *fly!*

First he must slip down from the tree carefully, quietly—and wait. Wait until he could hear them entering the copse. He went through the motions like a sleepwalker. His mind was numb. He kept telling himself—not when you hear their footsteps, not even when you hear their talking, but when the underbrush begins to scratch and tremble and you actually see them entering the thicket. Then —then run. Fly when the thicket and the woods can hide their view of you on the meadow.

His feet touched the ground, and he crouched under the lowest branches on all fours. He could hear them now, climbing the barrier of logs. The dog was whining, breathing frantically. Hans, searching out a break in the foliage, crept forward, trying not to move or snap a twig. His heart pounded in his ears. Every moment he waited for the gunshot . . . the teeth of the hound in his neck.

At last he heard them picking, then thrashing, at the underbrush to make a path. Now it was time.

With a swift lunge, he pushed himself free of the last branch. Not looking back, he furiously ran through the long grass. Though the air blew on him and he felt the cold grass whip his wet trousers, he shook as if he were burning alive in the molten, silver night. The dog barked but he couldn't look back; he couldn't do anything to slow his speed. He could see the tall reeds clearly now. Soon the ground turned soggy under his feet. Suddenly one shoe sank down into the mud and he fell. Dislodging his foot, he felt a twinge of pain in his ankle. On hands and knees, he crawled the last yard into the shelter of reeds that closed above his head. Kneeling cautiously, he peered back through the fronds.

At first he saw only shimmering grass all the way back to the thicket. It was a wider thicket than he had realized, curving around the back of the meadow to the forest close to his left. He found

the tall pine he had climbed. A moment later dog and soldiers pushed their way out by that tree. Hans' muscles tensed again. Now they had his scent. He must start swimming before they reached the riverbank. While they paused, he tried to put weight on his foot. He could barely do it and stand the pain. On all fours, he pushed his way down the bank. He could smell the muddy water. He crouched for a last look. They were coming at a rapid walk, the dog straining them faster on his taut chain.

With a deep breath, Hans slipped into the water. To his surprise, it felt warm, and he struck out for the other bank about twenty yards off. If I can only get halfway before they are halfway to me. For a second he felt giddy and light. He pushed his arms strongly in a breast stroke, but as he gathered his legs and kicked back, his foot gave him sharp pain. He stopped to recover, looking back in panic. He would have to do this slowly or not at all. After two more tries, he knew they would reach the bank before he could swim to the other side.

Turning back, he swam with a side stroke that favored his sprained ankle. He heaved himself up the bank and crouched in the reeds as he heard their voices. They appeared above him, farther down the bank at the place he had just left. The dog was barking and pawing the ground, trying to pull them down the bank.

"Come on, Dart, boy. Good boy, we can see better from here."

Frozen to the spot, Hans realized how right they were. If only he hadn't left the water! Its darkness would have hidden him. As they talked to themselves, gesturing, one followed the dog down the bank and the other got out his glasses.

Moving first one foot, then the other, Hans inched back over the edge of the bank on his hands and knees and slipped into the water. It was cold this time and it was hard to keep his teeth from chattering. Clamping his mouth shut, he floated, motionless, clutching some reeds. His eyes were glued to the soldiers and their hound.

At the place where Hans had first left the land, the dog sniffed and whined. Beams of a flashlight seared the dark reeds. One struck the spot right beside his fingers. Hans did not breathe. For the second time, the light arced away and then back. Hans took a sudden breath and sank under water.

Holding it as long as he could, he came up slowly, turning his face away from them. He could see the amber shade of light through the water. It swept over his head and then it was gone.

"Say—come up here," a voice called from above. Over the reeds, he saw the soldier and the dog climbing the bank in front of him. The second soldier stood at the top, shining his light on a long, black object that looked like a big automobile. Hans could just see a roof and some windows.

"What a joke!" said the soldier with the dog. "An old highway bus junked out here. See, here's writing on it . . ." The light dimmed as they bent over their flashlights.

Now's my chance, thought Hans.

Numb enough not to feel cold, he pushed into the river. The bank on the other side was yards away. With a breast stroke, he moved silently. His ankle didn't hurt as much. He looked behind once and saw the light combing the grass by the bus. Another five yards and he'd be there. He breathed more easily.

Then a sudden eerie cry, half squeal, half howl, came from the bank ahead.

Hans' breath stopped. What was that? The water

between him and the bank began moving. Another squealing cry—like a child or some wild animal? Suddenly a glare of light surrounded him in a blinding circle from the sky. The Mayerling Light? He saw a pointed, hairy face ahead—an animal struggling in the water—the open, yelping mouth with jagged teeth, like a fox. He stopped. In a moment the animal would be on him, tearing at him with his teeth. Again the flash of light. Now Hans saw two curly ears drooping by the jowl. A dog! A puppy with electric eyes of terror. Yelping, the dog tried to get on Hans' shoulder, scratching with its nails. Suddenly dizzy with relief, Hans swam forward, trying to shove the tubby body on his back. As he reached the bank a soldier waited with a pistol in his hand.

"Who goes there?"

Hans couldn't answer for a moment. He climbed out, staring, with the puppy under his arm. This was not one of the two soldiers. His uniform was different.

"I'm—uh—Hans, uh—Starrholm."

A flashlight covered his face. The slippery dog trembled in his arms and put its wet nose behind Hans' ear.

44

"What are you doing in the river this time of night?"

"This dog—" he tried to think—"my puppy— he ran away—my new pup. And now I found him in the river. He was drowning." Hans pulled the wet little face up to cover his own, stroking the dripping ears.

"Nice hound pup." The soldier patted the dog's head and put away his gun.

"Where do you live?" His voice was not suspicious.

Hans looked past his shoulder. He saw lights beyond the forest. "Up there—Mayerling Village."

"Okay then, lad." Out went the flashlight as he pocketed it. "Go on home then, you and your pup." He tweaked one of the dog's wet ears. "And don't go swimming at night in the river unless you want to be picked up by the Mayerling Light." He grinned, patting Hans on the shoulder.

"No, sir. Thank you, sir." Gripping the dog tightly, Hans hurried for the road, his ankle hurting. He was on the other side of the wall.

IV

H ANS stayed close to the walls of the joined houses. Their jutting roofs sliced a shadow from the moonlit alley in which he hid. Except for some trash barrels and a bicycle propped by a door, there were no signs of life. But in the distance he could hear the murmur of a crowd and an occasional whistle or the rumble of military vehicles. So far he had avoided the busy streets and no one had seen him.

A cat jumped up on a fence suddenly, and Hans' heart skipped a beat.

He could not walk very fast because of his throbbing ankle. And he still carried the wet puppy. On the road through Mayerling Village past the for-

47

est, he had tried to get rid of the puppy. Setting it down, he whispered hard, "Go home." But the little dog only wiggled its hind end, looking up at him. When Hans tried to run he followed him, yelping. Afraid the noise would attract attention, he snatched the puppy up. "Be quiet, *you!*" he said, shaking it. But the warm body was comforting against his ribs.

He hurried on now, down more side streets. An old man with a long loaf of bread and a suitcase scuttled past him in the alley. Later he heard a woman's voice crying, "Liza, where are you? Liza! Liza!" over and over. Several times a night watchman walked by a street lamp at a corner. But Hans ducked back, taking another detour. He should be getting near Hannah's after the next turn. What would he do when he got there? He must see her alone without her bossy aunt. His mother had never trusted the woman because she worked for the Party.

How would he get into their house on the second floor? And if his mother was not there, would Hannah tell him the truth about where she had gone and why the police suspected her?

But if Hannah and her no-good father were the

cause of the suspicion, would Hannah want to help him find his mother? Of course she would. She wouldn't want to lose that food his mother brought every week.

Crossing several more streets, Hans limped down the alley between Hannah's house and the one next to it. He crept into the back courtyard and crouched behind a bush. The dog shivered a little, then whimpered. *"Ssh!"* He pushed the puppy's nose under his arm. The houses surrounding the court were black and still. Moonlight fell across the uncut grass and bushes around the walls.

From Hannah's window above him, there was an orange glow behind the shade. She was awake! But how to get up there? At a corner of the house he saw the dark strip of a drainpipe going up the wall past her balcony. There was only one thing to do. Climb.

He set the puppy down, kneeling in front of it. "Now listen, you." He held the shaggy face between his hands. "You've got to be quiet. Understand?" The puppy whined at him, cocking its head. Hans smiled. "You're Kookie, y'know it? That's a good name or you." He patted the curly

49

ears. The puppy licked his cheek with a bristly tongue. "Now look, Kookie—*ssh*—be quiet till I get back." The puppy stood up, wagging its tail as Hans walked over to the drainpipe. He wrapped his legs around it and jerked himself up. The pipe wobbled and clanked. His ankle throbbed as it pressed down; he closed his eyes and pushed up again. When he opened them, he was barely two feet off the ground but he felt dizzy. The puppy yipped when Hans looked down. *"Ssh,"* he said, pointing to the ground. Kookie lay down.

Closing his eyes, Hans kept pushing up till his fingers touched the window box. With relief, he worked himself onto the edge, crowded with marigold and pansies. Swinging his legs over, he crouched down on the balcony.

Through the open casement, he could see into the small room lit by one candle on a table between a chair and the bed. In a white nightgown, Hannah stood by her bureau. There were some red flowers on it.

She's so little, Hans thought, not even as tall as I am.

Her long hair, gold in the candlelight, hung over her face. She was stirring something in a bowl. Two cats arched themselves against her legs, a black one behind her was mewing.

Turning, her hair fell back from the delicate face with its big, shadowed eyes. Her skin looked glassy white where it pulled close to the pointed nose and cheekbones. The gray eyes stared off to one side, thinking. Then, remembering the cats, she smiled. "*Ssh*, you silly geese, it's ready, *ssh!*" She giggled softly, carrying the bowl to her bedside.

Then she went back to her bureau. Pushing things aside in a drawer, she took out a large bag and carried it over to the bed. She sat down, poured out dozens of small chocolate balls, and began sorting them into several paper bags. Her fingers were like a child's, but she worked quickly and with energy, stopping to listen now and then.

She is afraid someone will find her. No wonder, with all that candy!

Suddenly Hannah straightened up, her fingers to her mouth. Putting the last chocolates into a bag, she snatched them up and ran to what looked like a lamp with a black shade in the corner. Raising the shade—it was a black piece of cloth—she stuffed the bags between the bars of a bird cage. As she came back to the bed there was a knock at

the door. "Come in," she called in a wavering voice, and picked up the cats' bowl.

"Hannah! You up at this hour?" Her aunt walked in, a tall glum woman in a dark robe. "What are you doing, child?" Her black eyes glanced over the room. For a moment, Hannah did not turn around. Then she slowly limped to the bureau, setting down the bowl.

"Oh, Auntie, it's just the animals. You know Cinder's been sick. He needs more food. And then the other two have to have a bit, too—you know . . ." She laughed, nervously pouring something into the bowl.

"But, Hannah, why must you do this in the middle of the night? With lights on at this hour? What will the block leader think!"

"But, Auntie, it isn't using electricity—it's just a candle."

The woman came across the room. "I know, dear, but it's dangerous! The minute I'm not around at night, you're out of bed!" She blew out the candle and turned on the table lamp. "Oh, Hannah, not more flowers!"

"Auntie, take them please. They are for you." Hannah limped over with the bouquet.

53

"Oh thank you, dear." The aunt set them on the table, smiling. She stroked Hannah's cheek and then held up her chin. "But something much more important, young lady. You didn't put the beans to soak for tomorrow."

"Oh!" Hannah clapped her hand to her mouth. "I'm sorry. I forgot. But it's only Monday."

"Why do you always forget when I'm not home?" The aunt sighed. "Sorry to miss supper. We all worked late—emergency business." She yawned and rubbed her forehead. "Oh, I'm tired."

"Poor auntie. I'm sorry about the beans. But I just got picking these flowers and I forgot. But, Auntie, honestly, tell me. Don't you think that sometimes looking at flowers is more important? It even gives you more energy than eating beans. Don't you?" She looked at her aunt with bright eyes.

"Oh, Hannah!" The woman leaned toward the geraniums. "They're nice." She closed her eyes and sniffed. "But"—the long cheeks sagged again— "one can't eat flowers. Hannah, what do you have in the cats' bowl?" She walked to the bureau. "*What!* Feeding those animals your own meat ration! Oh, Hannah, you are impossible." She

54

pressed her thin lips together. "No wonder you look so pale. By the way"—she looked serious—"did your Aunt Maria come with the vegetables today?"

Hannah turned to the flowers on the table. Her hands hovered over them and her eyes looked down. "Oh yes, yes! She brought them." Her voice was jerky, and she forced a yawn. "Oh, I'm sleepy too."

"She did not speak of any—trouble or—"

"Trouble? Oh no," Hannah said quickly. She knelt down to stroke the cats.

"Well, they'll be stricter about some things now —with the wall—"

"The wall?" Hannah stood up to face her aunt.

"Now, Hannah, you know we've always talked of this. And tonight orders were given to begin building it." The aunt steadied her voice. "It's only for awhile—only to keep out unfriendly people and to keep our own people at home doing their jobs."

"But a wall dividing up the whole city so no one can come and go any more!"

Her aunt towered over her but her voice was patient. "Your Aunt Maria can still visit you with her pass and bring us food. I'll see to that myself."

"It isn't fair." Hannah's voice shook. "People should be able to come and go if they don't like it here!"

"*Ssh.*" The woman put her finger over Hannah's mouth and smoothed her forehead. "Oh, child, why can't you learn?" She patted her cheek, looking at her deeply. "You can't build a new world if people won't work together, or if they can't face hard times for awhile."

Hannah turned her back, looking down with wide eyes.

"You know, Hannah, if you really loved your country and your people, you'd try to forget the past—you'd try to change." She gently turned Hannah around and smiled. "You'd give up your silly notions—your flowers and animals. And take care of yourself and work for the Party."

Hannah looked at her. "I'll never forget—the past." She lowered her voice. "But I'll try and mend my ways."

There was a long silence except for the sound of the animals licking themselves.

"But I don't want to change—I don't want to forget, ever. My father said, 'There's nothing to be afraid of except being afraid.' " Hannah looked up again. "But now with the wall, I am afraid."

The aunt shook her head, watching Hannah patiently. "There's nothing fearful in a wall. It's a practical step for now." Walking to Hannah's bed, she drew back the sheet. "You have to be practical in this world, Hannah. You've got to live in the present, dear. Now come to bed." Hannah slowly got under the covers. "Goodnight, Hannah." The aunt bent down and kissed her. The light went off.

"Good night, Aunt," Hannah murmured.

Hans stared at the black window. What should he think of Hannah now? At least she had a mind of her own and she thought the way he did about the wall. Could she be trusted? He waited a few moments, then quietly tapped on the windowpane.

V

"HANNAH?" he whispered. Her white face appeared at the casement.

"Oh, Hans!" She opened the window.

He slipped onto the moonlit floor beside her.

Hannah looked at him, standing motionless and seeming as white as stone. "What's the matter?"

For a moment he didn't answer, feeling the pleasure of warmth, seeing the rosy blanket on her bed, the animals curled up there, sleeping. He gritted his teeth to keep them from chattering suddenly.

"My mother, she never came home tonight."

Hannah drew in her breath, clasping her face with both hands. "Oh no . . ."

"Hannah, where is she?"

"But, Hans, I don't know. She came at the usual time and left as usual. She said she was going home."

"But which way did she go? I went to the bridge where she usually crosses." He searched her staring face.

"You're so wet, Hans. What happened?" She touched his sleeve.

"I swam the river, that's what. The guards chased me over the Mayerling River." He spoke impatiently.

Hannah's eyes were dark and still. "You were chased by *soldiers?*"

"Yes, later, to get over here. Because I couldn't find Mother at the bridge. No one was being allowed to cross. What could have happened to her?"

Black rims showed under Hannah's eyes. Why didn't she say something?

"And there was this officer"—Hans' voice sharpened—"who had Mother's name on some list."

Hannah's eyes looked past him into the shadows.

"And he said they are watching for her and she'd better be telling the truth about bringing you food."

Now she was looking at him.

60

"Hannah, what is the truth? It's because of your father, isn't it? He did something bad and had to go to prison, didn't he? My mother is in danger because of him. That officer said, 'You have quite some black sheep for relatives'!"

"My father went to prison honorably, Hans." Hannah spoke suddenly, moonlight shining from the darkness of her eyes, and her face proud. "You must believe that"—she lowered her voice—"but I can't tell you more, not now."

"No, not until my mother gets arrested too, is that it?"

"Oh no, Hans, of course not." She sounded hurt.

"Then tell me where to go now. So I can find her. Tell me—"

"Wait, Hans." Hannah touched his arm gently. "I know the way she went and you must not follow her—not yet. It is not safe." Her voice was quiet.

Hans was angry. "Listen, you! Just because you're a year older than me don't think you are going to give me orders."

She touched his shoulder, trying to smile, and he suddenly felt tired. Her slippers scuffed the floor as she walked toward the bureau. Pulling some clothes from a drawer, she came toward him.

61

"Hans, excuse me, I'm sorry for the way I spoke." He couldn't see her face in the shadows. "We must talk together. When you are warm and dry, we can talk better." She held the things out to him.

Half angry, half embarrassed, he took the clothes and went where she pointed, through the door of the bathroom. He knew he'd been rude, too, but just the same! She certainly knew where his mother had gone. Why wouldn't she tell him? And what else did she know? He shivered, feeling cold tiles under his bare feet. But the wool of her slippers, the warmth of the shirt and trousers, covered him like a warm skin. Perhaps Hannah wasn't so bad; perhaps she had reasons for secrecy. He opened the door.

From the shadows by the bird cage, she turned toward him, her robe gathered up in front of her. As she entered the moonlight, he saw the paper bags inside the folds.

"Outside the window, I saw you before, hiding those chocolate balls! My mother brought them to you, didn't she?"

Hannah nodded.

Hans set his jaw angrily. "Do you realize how my mother pinches and saves to bring you food—

our own carrots and lettuce and apples from one poor little garden—and now candy! It's disgusting. And I don't even believe you're sick. I saw you limping in front of your aunt, but you're well enough now! And you let my mother bring you free pills from her own pharmacy!"

Hannah nodded slowly. "Yes, Hans." She walked to the bed, dumping down the bags. Pointing to the chair, she said quietly, "Sit down please." She pulled out a chocolate ball. "I would like you to have one."

"No thank you!" He stood over her.

"I want you to see for yourself what's in them," she said, pushing it into his hand. What was she driving at? He put the ball in his mouth. The creamy stuff tasted of chocolate at first, but then a bitterness stung his tongue. He spat it out into his hand, looking at the white tablet.

"Phew! It tastes like an aspirin."

"That's what it is. And see this darker shade?" She held up another. "This one is penicillin."

"But it sure looks like chocolate." He stared at her.

She nodded, smiling now. "The guards thought so too."

"But why, what for?"

"They aren't for me, Hans. As you said, I'm not sick, but many in our parish are really ill. Since it's illegal to bring in medicine, your mother thought of putting it in candy." The rims below Hannah's eyes were darker now and there was an excited look on her face. "People are hungry too. There just isn't enough food to go around any more. I give away most of your mother's fruit and vegetables. I take the medicine to the pastor of our church secretly. And he gives it to the parish doctors."

"So that's why she brings such a lot."

Hannah nodded. "My aunt thinks I'm sick, so she gets permission for your mother to bring extra food. She doesn't know about the pills. But now . . ." She frowned, sitting down.

"What now?"

"Well, last week the border guards were more suspicious. They looked under the vegetables in the false bottom of your mother's sack and found the smuggled bottles and pillboxes and took them away. And they warned your mother not to bring them again. They know she has a pharmacy."

"But they let her through, didn't they?"

"Yes, last week it was all right. But this week,

although they let her pass, she thinks she was followed here by a man in a dark suit with a cane."

"But why would someone follow her if they let
her through all right? It doesn't make sense."

"Oh, Hans, you don't know." She stood up,
clasping her hands, walking away and back again.
"It's not unusual to have people snooping around,
once you're under suspicion. That's why we have
to be so careful. We might lead them to where she
is."

"Under suspicion? I don't see why it's so suspicious to bring medicines and food over here when
you haven't enough of them anyway!"

"Because it reminds our people of your side of
the wall where you can get these good things. And
it makes them want to go away from here." She
leaned toward him. "You see"—she spoke more
slowly—"if anyone is caught bringing things when
they're not allowed to, well—that person—well,
it's dangerous."

"Dangerous, you mean my mother could be arrested!"

"No, Hans—we don't know that yet—"

"My mother could have been arrested! So she
came this week just the same with even more pills

disguised as chocolate!" Hans felt his anger re-turning. "What if they found out? How could she dare take the risk? Hannah! It's your fault. Why did you let her do it?" He glared at her.

She looked away, taking a deep breath. "I used to argue, Hans," she said with effort, "and since it has gotten dangerous I begged her to stop—for your sake." Her fingers pulled at her collar. "But others have worked in spite of danger—she can't forget them. Neither of us can." She looked away again.

"Others who worked—in spite of danger? What have they to do with my mother, a poor woman without a husband, scrimping and saving and working hard to earn a living?"

Hannah looked at him with softness in her face. "I know, Hans. And she thinks of you always. And what your—father would have wanted."

"What my father wanted?"

She nodded, biting her lip. Tails of hair fell over her cheeks as she looked down.

Was she crying? Embarrassed, Hans turned toward the window. The moon was falling, cut in half by a roof across the courtyard. Mist veiled the sleeping houses.

Suddenly he felt impatient. "What has my father to do with all this?"

For a moment Hannah covered her face with her hands. Then she looked up. "Oh, Hans, I'm sorry for telling it this way. I didn't mean to say so much."

"But don't try to hide anything *now*."

She shook her head. "Of course not. I didn't mean that." Then, staring beyond Hans, her face lost expression; it was blank except for her eyes. She spoke in a monotone.

"Long ago—your father and mine knew that the leader of the Party was not a good man. Secretly, in cellars and attics of houses, they met with people telling them how to object and vote against him." She stood with her arms folded on her chest, as if to calm herself. "Then finally—eight years ago—you and I were too little to know—during a raid by the police most of the others escaped, but my father stayed behind. Your father got a bad wound in his side"—she swallowed—"and could not leave." She looked down. "And he died. Then my father was caught and sent away into exile."

She kept on talking but Hans didn't hear any

68

more. He shuddered. Taking a few steps backward, he found the chair. His own father shot in a cellar. And Hannah's father sent to prison for life. There was a kind of roaring in his head. He couldn't seem to hear what Hannah was saying.

She crouched beside him, her hand on his shoulder.

Staring at her, he heard himself say, "Oh, Mother, Mother, why didn't you tell me! I should have known."

"Hans, your mother was right to keep it secret. It is not safe for you to know the truth. Your mother was afraid for you. It's dangerous for all of us who work in the underground. Even I have not been told everything about the medicines—who gets them or how. I only know that there are workers all over the city bringing things over, and others taking them where they're needed." Her voice was trembling. "But we have to be careful. Police are always on the lookout. They watch you. All my life they have been watching me."

He looked at her drawn face swaying in front of him, felt her fingers pressing his arm.

"You must promise to forget every word I have told you. Promise, Hans, promise. Nothing, nothing must happen to you and your mother. My tru-est, dearest friends in all this rotten world." Then she leaned on his shoulder, crying.

Somehow the sound eased the pounding of his heart. At last Hans said, "Hannah, don't cry, please don't cry. We just have to find a way. We have to find my mother and get her out of danger and bring her back . . ."

After a moment Hannah looked at him. "Oh I'm sorry, Hans, for crying—for telling you like this." She stood up, wiping her eyes. "It's such a relief to tell someone." She smoothed her hair back, taking a breath. "In the morning it should be safe to follow her. After Aunt has gone to work, we can slip away and follow her new route. Your mother was going to try a new check point where the gate guards would not know her and be so suspicious."

"And if she isn't there?"

"We'll ask the Pastor to help us. I have to bring him the medicine as usual tomorrow at the church. Perhaps he can think of something."

VI

HANS woke as daylight came through a crack in the door. He was lying on the floor, a feather quilt around him like a cocoon. The air of Hannah's closet smelled of potatoes and dried flowers. It reminded him of the crushed herbs in his mother's apothecary jars. Mother! He swallowed the lump in his throat. Where was she now? Would he ever find her? He sat up. If only she had told him everything: that gunshot in a cellar far away; his father dead and Hannah's father taken prisoner.

A wet nose sniffed, then licked his face. Kookie!

He rubbed his cheek on the woolly head. "Well, now we know and we're going to find Mother and get her back again."

He spoke savagely between his teeth while he pushed open the door. "Good morning, Hannah."

She looked like another person by daylight. A straight, dark smock replaced the soft robe. The silken hair was drawn into straw-colored pigtails. And freckles showed on her nose between the matter-of-fact eyes.

"Your own clothes are dry now, Hans." She spoke quickly, winding the braids around her head. "And I saved you some things for breakfast."

He nodded, wishing she would smile, and went into the bathroom.

More at ease in his own shirt and pants, he ate the bread, cheese and apple she had set on the table for him. There was a bowlful for Kookie. Silently, Hannah folded the quilt, put it in the closet, and brought out a bulging bag.

"The candy is for the Pastor," she said, almost gaily.

Her white eyebrows puckered thoughtfully as she fastened the buckles. "Hans, we mustn't walk together. I mean side by side—in case anyone follows us. That man who followed your mother might know me, since he followed her here."

Hans nodded.

"Luckily we can ride most of the way." She handed him a ticket. "But you stay at least three yards behind wherever I go."

"But where are we going?"

"*Ssh!* Someone might hear you through the walls." She strapped the bag over her shoulder, tying a scarf around her head. "The less you know the better. But we'll go to Fortinbras Gate. Your mother was going to try that way home, to see if the guards were easier."

"Then what?" he whispered.

"Just look around for her and listen to the talk at the barrier. There'll be an awful lot of people asking an awful lot of questions today." She pulled on a coat. "And remember, Hans"—her voice was firm—"you don't know me or remember anything at all of what I said last night. Your name is Hans Jordan and you lost your pass swimming the river to rescue your dog." Her voice scolded him but she held up two fingers, crossed for good luck. And she smiled.

Down in the street it was not easy to keep Hannah in sight and stay well behind her. Cars, bicycles and pedestrians hurried past him, blocking his view. Kookie trotted by his heels.

At the far end of the street, where it joined a square, he saw two policemen gesturing at the crowd. Some soldiers standing in an armored car and looking ahead through binoculars drove past the intersection.

Hans' throat felt dry and his legs began to tremble. Under his breath he said, Hannah, don't go this way. No more soldiers, no more policemen, please. Then he saw her blue-scarfed head bobbing gradually off to the right.

Pushing his way behind her through the traffic, he crossed the street. He felt safer now, taking this back alley between two rows of houses. There was nothing between Hannah and himself except ash barrels and Kookie, pattering ahead.

But soon Hans felt uneasy passing under the rows of open windows. No faces appeared, but the distant sounds of a radio, a telephone ringing, the slam of a door, reminded him that at any moment someone could look out and spot them easily. He looked behind to be sure there was no one following. He tried not to hurry, but he noticed that Hannah was almost running up the slight incline.

From a doorway just behind her, an old man with grizzled hair under his dark beret walked out, tapping his way ahead with the white cane of a blind man. Kookie ran up to him, barking, until the old man turned around to glare with his vacant eyes. Shuddering, Hans called Kookie, who ran back growling, his tail between his legs. The blind man tapped his way faster up the alley.

Reaching the end of it, Hannah thrust herself into the crowd by the trolley stop. The blind man disappeared around the corner. Trying to keep his distance, Hans pretended to tie his shoe as a trolley rolled to a halt. Passengers hung from the windows, jammed along the aisle, and overflowed down the steps at the rear. Were he and Hannah going to ride on this?

But the people quickly oozed out of the doors and down the hill to the left in a wide stream. Below them in the distance, Hans saw hundreds more, like black midgets swarming along the wall which cut across the center of the great square. Jeeps and armored cars rolled back and forth. Policemen waved their arms at street corners where people continued to stream by them. Hans could hear the distant blare of the public-address system.

With relief, he saw Hannah climb onto the trolley. He took Kookie under one arm and followed her. Hannah chose a seat up front; Hans sat down in the rear. He felt relieved. Hannah was going to be in one place for awhile. No more than half the seats were taken, and it would be easy to see when she got off. The trolley clanged away, and the conductor took his ticket.

Time passed in a series of stops and starts. Now passengers got on and no one got off. After all the seats were taken, people stood in the aisles. Frantically, Hans realized that he couldn't see Hannah through the crush of heads and shoulders. He should have moved closer before. Taking Kookie, who wriggled to get free, he tried to push his way through. But he only got dark looks and grunts, so he sat down again.

Soon they left the city behind them. He could see the white sky above the empty fields. How far were they going? How much longer would it be till they got there?

At last the trolley stopped by a sign, FORTINBRAS GATE, on the roof of a station platform. He pushed ahead with his elbows but the whole crowd pushed

too. Hannah disappeared down the steps of the car. Hans couldn't find her blue scarf on the crowded platform.

Through the front window, Hans saw a striped pole blocking the trolley tracks ahead. A guard was checking the papers of some people waiting there. On the wall of the sentry house there was another sign: WARNING: BORDER LINE. NO MORE PASSING THIS CHECK POINT WITHOUT SPECIAL PERMISSION. INQUIRE STATION HOUSE.

Hans felt himself pulled down the steps of the car by the tide of people. They pushed back along the platform, behind the trolley and across the tracks to a meadow. On the edge of it he stopped to watch. Like some dark herd, they ran by him up along the barbed wire fence that stretched far across the meadow. Others already there looked around and made space for them. Hands waved from the other side, there were sobs and little cries of recognition. And then bunched together they talked in low tones across the barrier, some glancing sideways at the soldier. Others just stood there staring.

Hans went closer. All these dark shoulders looked alike. He put Kookie down and walked slowly among the huddled figures, peering at every face. He could feel a tightening in his throat. His mother was not there.

He turned back across the road looking for Hannah. As the trolley pulled away he found her in the crowd by the station house. One finger pointed for him to go inside.

Pushing up the steps through the people he looked into a dingy room lit by one bulb. People waited in a line leading to a grilled window usually used for selling tickets. The sign above it read: EMERGENCY BORDER PERMIT.

A woman with a basket on her arm was talking there. ". . . for my daughter. I only wanted to bring her eggs." There was a pause. "Just eggs." Her voice was shrill. "I'll come right back."

She almost shook her fist. But a nearby guard took her arm, showing her out a side exit onto the platform.

Next a man in overalls handed a paper through the window. There were low questions and answers. A hand behind the grille loudly stamped something. The workman turned around, a paper trembling in his hands. "But it's where I work, my job." He spoke to the crowd with frozen staring

79

eyes. Again the guard stepped up pointing to the exit. The workman's face sagged and suddenly he looked old.

Several more went out that way. One man shaking with anger, another woman crying. But most of them walked with their eyes down, lips in a pencil line, the color gone from their faces. Hans didn't want to see anymore. The room smelled of old varnish and people squeezed against him so he couldn't breathe.

Now a young woman was speaking quietly. "But I've already told you I only came for a visit with a permit. I want to go home."

"We suspect . . ." Hans couldn't catch the rest of the words.

The young woman shook her black curls. "No, nothing."

"Guard," the officer called, his face pushing above the grille.

A soldier came from the back of the room and led the girl away by the arm. The officer spoke louder facing the crowd, "Any visitors from the other side, you may as well go away for now. You'll be allowed back home eventually. But not today, we've too much work." He pulled his ear impatiently. "Do you understand—maybe to-morrow."

The crowd listened but they were watching the young woman look over her shoulder piteously for help. The soldier opened a door marked BAGGAGE. When it closed after her, a bolt fell into place. A kind of gasp went through the line and people turned and looked at each other.

Someone pulled at Hans' sleeve. Startled he swung around. With relief he saw it was Hannah. "Let's get away," she scarcely breathed in his ear. He pushed his way back down the steps. Why should they go now? Perhaps his mother was in that room. They should wait and find out.

The platform was crowded. No one moved about. Nobody was talking. Hannah stopped some distance from Hans turning to stare at the dirt road behind them. She looked as if she were watching for something. He wanted to talk to her, and tell her not to go. But he didn't dare in front of the people. Perhaps he could signal to her when the trolley came.

He looked for Kookie but there was no sign of him. The field across the tracks was empty except for the dark figures still huddled along the barrier.

81

Then he heard barking behind the station house. He walked back there slowly to avoid attention. As he almost reached the corner he heard another sharp yip, as if from pain. Then Kookie's tail end appeared backing away from the building. Finally his head showed. He was growling and held one end of a white stick in his teeth. The person pulling at the other end was hidden behind the house.

Suddenly the motor of a heavy vehicle roared on. Hans crouched down, calling to Kookie under the sound. He dropped the stick joyfully and ran to Hans. Picking up the dog, he saw a bruise on its nose. Who would hurt a little dog like that? The stick had vanished.

He edged to the corner of the building carefully. Something told him to keep out of sight. Then he quickly glanced around the back. A soldier was slamming the rear doors of a big truck. Hans saw that it was crowded with people. And the blind man (now he remembered him back in the alley near Hannah's house) nodded to the soldier and tapped away with his white cane. Hans watched the truck pull away down the road, wondering.

Putting Kookie down, he went back to the platform to find Hannah. The blind man, making his way through the crowd, stopped near her. But she didn't notice, nor did she turn at the sound of the trolley. She kept on staring at the truck—now a speck in the distance.

VII

O N the trolley going back, Hans was surprised to see Hannah get off before they reached the city. Behind some other passengers, he followed her out into a wooded park. Kookie trotted about, sniffing the grass. Through the trees, Hans saw Hannah picking flowers in a field.

Making sure that no one saw him, he caught up with her. "What are you doing! Don't you have any plan about finding that truck with the prisoners? Maybe Mother's on it."

Hannah nodded. "But aren't you hungry?" She smiled, looking at her flowers, and he got even angrier.

"No, I hadn't even thought of it! I want to keep going till we find out something . . ."

85

Hannah knelt on the grass and removed the bag from under her coat.

"I do, too, but we've got to eat. And besides, I didn't dare go to the Pastor at the church, because I think we are being followed by that man with a blind man's cane. He got on the trolley for Fortinbras Gate and he was always somewhere nearby." She handed him bread and cheese.

"That man with the cane who followed Mother —do you think he's the one?"

"Yes, I do. So just as we came to the trolley stop for church, I decided not to get off. Then *he* got off!" She took a bite of bread and cheese.

"Well now, what do we do?" Hans' bread and cheese tasted dry.

Hannah frowned as she ate. "I will go to the church with the medicine—the Pastor will be expecting me—and ask for any news of the prison truck and your mother. But, Hans"—she looked serious—"you must go back to my room and wait."

"Go back and wait? Why?"

"Well, because if that man is a spy, if I'm alone it will be easier to avoid him. With two of us, it would be harder and more dangerous."

"But, Hannah, I want to go. It's my mother."

"I know, Hans. I want to find your mother just as much as you do—and that's what we're doing, but it's dangerous and we have to be careful." She picked up the flowers. "And it's more than that, Hans. If we are caught with the medicine, well— not even thinking about ourselves—if we are caught it will hurt many people."

"What do I care about them!" He said quickly but his own words stung him.

Hannah fingered the flowers. "This way, if I don't come back pretty soon, you can go to the church later and check on me. See the Pastor. No one would suspect you at all."

Hans couldn't answer for a moment. He tried to think fairly.

"I know, Hannah." His voice was small. "And I'm sorry for the way I spoke. But look"—the idea came to him suddenly—"since no one would suspect me, you just said it yourself, *I'm* the one to go to the church, because it's you—a girl—that man is looking for. Don't you see?" His breath came short; he must convince her.

"No, Hans. No!" She touched his hand, her eyes soft. "Your mother would never forgive me if anything went wrong. She didn't want you mixed up in any of this."

Suddenly his throat felt choked and he blinked hard. "But don't you see I want to be mixed up in it? It isn't fair; my mother should have let me help." Unable to speak, he leaned over to pat Kookie.

Hannah's voice was strained. "But, Hans, you can help. By waiting to see if I need help. And if I don't succeed, then you can try."

He stared at the flowers in her lap, his eyes filling. Why should he wait? Every moment was time lost from finding his mother. He looked at the bag on the grass between them. Slipping two fingers around the strap, he pulled it toward him.

"No, Hannah, we mustn't wait. Each minute counts. I'm going to the Pastor. And you're going to tell me how to do it." She looked up, startled, as he removed his jacket sleeve, hung the strap on his shoulder, and buttoned the jacket again.

"Hans, no." She stood up, dropping the flowers. "Be sensible. I can't tell you how to go—it's too hard."

"Then, Hannah, you come. Just lead me, the way we did before. I'll stay far behind, and you go by the church and keep going. If anyone stops you

—well, you aren't carrying anything you shouldn't. You're doing an errand. Here"—he picked up the flowers—"carry these. You're taking them to a friend." She looked at him, round-eyed.

"Oh, Hans!" She breathed a little sigh and smiled. "Do you think it would really work?" Then the smile faded. "But, Hans, if they stop us and search us—?"

His head felt light as he stood up. "Why should they? If it looks dangerous, keep on walking." He tried to hide his sudden uneasiness by rubbing one arm and then the other. The air seemed very cold. "And I'll—I'll just come back here."

She looked at him seriously. "All right, Hans, I'll do it because it might work. But promise me— if that man with the cane is waiting, be sure he follows me before you go in the church. There's a door on each side and the main one is in the front. But I'll lead you to the church from the back, so we'll have a chance to look around. If anything looks unusual"—her voice tightened—"promise me to walk right by! We'll come back here and decide what to do."

"All right." He nodded soberly.

* * * * *

After fifteen minutes of walking, Hannah, a half block ahead of Hans, turned the corner. At the end of the street, he saw carved pillars in a half circle around the rear of a large stone church. Hannah kept on slowly, her flowers nodding over her shoulder. Then, reaching the end of the street, she waited at the intersection. After crossing, she went toward a little cemetery to the right. Turning down the path between it and the church, she stopped suddenly.

Standing at the curb, Hans saw what had stopped her—the wall! Coming from the right, it crossed the back of the cemetery lawn and cut in front of her path, joining itself to the church. It was three feet taller than Hannah. Only the tops of some poplars waved from behind it.

Backing up, Hannah walked toward him on the path. Halfway along, she tried a side door of the church. It didn't open. Coming toward him again, she went around to the back of the church. He waited again, turning to whistle at Kookie. When he looked back, Hannah hurried across the street and disappeared in a doorway to his left. He followed slowly, walking close to the buildings. What had brought her back so fast?

As he walked, he cautiously glanced across the

street at the far side of the church. The man with the cane was not there. Two boys were playing ball in a stone courtyard. The wall continued behind them, some workmen still cementing stones at the top. By a side door of the church, stood two soldiers in steel helmets with rifles on their backs! They watched the boys' game and talked together. Looking farther to the left and back to the right, Hans saw no one. He kept walking. What were he and Hannah to do now?

In a moment he saw Hannah beckoning from the shadowed entrance of a building. He slipped in beside her.

"Hans, the wall!" Her face seemed to shrink into the bones of her cheeks. "It has cut off the front of our church. Oh, what if something has happened to the Pastor!" She clung to his arm. "And the soldiers, what are they doing? The door on the cemetery side is locked. Those guards are standing in front of the only entrance on this side of the wall."

"Probably they're only guarding the wall. They do it on our side every few yards!" He softly whistled for Kookie, who panted up and lay down beside them. "Hannah!" Hans flattened himself against the wall of the building. "He's coming!"

Her lips turned white as she pressed back beside him. Between the passing cars and people, Hans recognized the gray hair under the beret. The man wore dark glasses now, and the white cane tapped in front of him. Stopping by the courtyard, he seemed to smell the air. Then, casually, he went over to the soldiers and spoke a few words. One of them looked at his watch, the old man nodded, said something and went on his way up the street.

Hannah and Hans looked at each other. "He only pretended to ask the time. He told them to look for me." Her eyes were round and dark. "Hans, you mustn't try to get in the church now. It's too dangerous. The soldiers will surely stop you."

Hans wasn't listening; he was trying to think. He mustn't get excited or do anything reckless. But somehow—there must be a way to get by those soldiers. If he could just get them away from the door. He looked at Hannah. He felt frightened as he spoke, but he must take the chance.

"Hannah, hold Kookie until I get in the church. Then walk back to the park. I'll meet you there."

"Hans—" She gasped, her fingers over her mouth.

92

"It's all right. The soldiers won't even see me."
Forcing himself onto the sidewalk, he crossed the
street. He slowed down and looked both ways as
he reached the church, but there was no sign of
the "blind" man. Hans put his hands in his pockets
and tried to whistle but he couldn't. Instead, he
found a pebble and skimmed it along the edge of
the courtyard. The soldiers turned around to look
at him. His legs began to tremble so much that he
leaned against the corner of the church.

"Say, can I play ball?" he called to the two boys.
They stopped and looked at each other. The nearest one, with freckles, winked at his friend in a blue
jacket by the wall.

"All right. You be in the middle and try to get
the ball away from us, see?" said the blue-jacketed
one.

"Yeah," said the freckled one, and they both
laughed.

As Hans ran into the middle, one soldier stared
at him, the other scratched his chin thoughtfully.
The ball went back and forth over his head. Even
if I jump, I won't get it, thought Hans. I'm too
short.

First, Hans faced the blue-jacketed boy and then

turning, jumped for the ball tossed by his freckle-faced friend. He saw one guard walk out to the street and look up and down. They're suspicious; maybe they're looking for Hannah. Better hurry. Meanwhile, the boys, seeing how easy it was to toss over Hans' head, began throwing it closer to him.

The next throw Hans lunged up and grabbed it.

"Aw gosh, I let you get that," said Freckle-face, blushing.

Hans took his place facing the wall and tossed to the other boy. He returned it over the head of his friend. Hans glanced back; both guards were again standing by the church door, talking. With a sudden fast peg, Hans threw the ball beyond the reach of the blue-jacketed boy. It landed on the top of the wall at the far end, rolling down the other side.

"Dumbbell!" shouted Freckle-face, and both boys headed for the wall. Vainly, Freckle-face tried to fit his toes into a crevice. Unable to climb up, he knelt down and let the other one stand on his back.

"Hey, stop that!" yelled a soldier.

"Get down from there," the other one called,

and they both hurried toward the wall. When their backs were turned, Hans ducked into the side door of the church.

It seemed dark at first, but there was still light enough for the guards to see him if they followed. Getting down on his hands and knees between the pews, Hans crawled toward the main aisle. The flagstones were cold and his scraped leg hurt him. It was very still. Straining his ears, he heard nothing outside. But any moment the door behind might open and he would hear heavy boots and angry voices.

He crept around behind a large pillar and stood up. It was awesome in the purplish light from the stained-glass windows, and the air smelled moldy. Over the backs of the worn, wooden benches, he looked toward the nave of the church. The pulpit box was empty behind the big, open Bible. The red-and-blue glass of the window behind cast a checkered pattern on the white altar cloth under the gold cross. Some roses drooped in a silver bowl.

There was no sign or sound of life anywhere. Turning around, he tiptoed down the aisle toward the shadows of what must be the main door cut off by the wall. The dank air penetrated his thin jacket, and it smelled as if moss grew in the shadow of the arched ceiling. Overhead, he could see where stones had come loose and sky showed through. The benches sagged with age, all the paint worn away in seats hollowed by centuries of praying.

Hans shivered. A church was a sad old place with nothing alive left in it.

Suddenly he stopped. He heard a shuffle of feet, a whisper beyond the last pew. He quickly slid behind a pillar.

A tall figure hesitated in the shadows. Dirt spotted his black gown and the white square of cloth was crooked under a tired face. The Pastor stared out over the pews. His kind mouth moved soundlessly as he bowed over his hands.

Hans wondered how to begin. There was something so old and beaten in the man—just like his poor church. As if nothing mattered any more.

Hans spoke softly, coming out into the aisle.

The Pastor dropped his hands slowly. "Yes, what is it?" His eyes widened. "Did the soldiers let you in?"

"No, I tricked them. Will they follow me?"

The Pastor nodded, quickly motioning Hans to

go with him. Inside a small room, he locked the door.

"Hannah sent me with these." Hans hastily undid the bag and pulled out the paper sacks. "Medicine from my mother's pharmacy."

"Ah, the medicine," the Pastor said quietly.

"Yes. Pills are inside this chocolate coating."

The Pastor put both hands on Hans' shoulders. "Bless you, my boy, bless you." His eyes were full. "Many people are living because of your mother's generosity and courage. And many will live because of what *you* have done today." Bowing his head, he muttered, "No walls a prison are for such a mighty wing, Oh Lord."

Hans felt embarrassed. Should he bow his head also?

"But, my boy." The Pastor looked up gravely. "You must leave here now. The soldiers will be coming. I have a way to put you through the wall."

"But, Pastor, my mother—do you know where she is?"

"Yes, I know." He nodded heavily. "They followed her from Hannah's house to the place she goes every week for instructions about next week's medicine. She was arrested."

"Arrested?" Hans' stomach gave a sickening lurch. "Where is she now?"

From the back of the church, they heard voices, the scrape of heavy boots.

"Quick." Pulling Hans behind him, the Pastor left the office, going through a curtain. The heavy entrance door creaked as the Pastor slowly pulled it open. Inches beyond the door, the entrance arch was filled from top to bottom with bricks and stones of different shapes and sizes.

"Stay here. Not a sound. I'll come again." Pushing Hans flat against the wall, the Pastor closed the great door behind him.

VIII

A T LAST the door creaked open.
"They've gone." The Pastor touched Hans'
shoulder, leading him back through the curtain.
"You must go home over the wall now, son," the
Pastor whispered hoarsely, his face in the shadow.
"The soldiers asked if a boy had come here."

"Did they see me?"

"No, but—"

"But I can't go home now without my mother!
Do you know where she is?"

The Pastor looked at his hands. "We've heard
that your mother and others were taken to the in-
fantry barracks in the Mayerling Forest. It is used
as a—detention camp."

"Detention camp?"

He nodded. "A place where they—keep people
a while for questioning—"

"You mean to find out if my mother will tell about, about the medicine?"

The Pastor nodded again.

"Oh, she won't tell. My mother would never do that." Then he stopped, his insides turning over. "But what will they do to her if she doesn't?"

"Listen, my boy, they don't have any proof." The Pastor put his hands on Hans' shoulder. "Most likely they'll only question your mother and release her. But if not we're trying to help everyone who is taken."

"But, Pastor, isn't there something I can do to help now?"

Patting Hans' shoulder, the Pastor dropped his hands.

"You can help, yes, by going back to safety. I have found a way through those stones in the church door. But you must go at once." He looked at Hans keenly. "And take Hannah with you."

"Is Hannah in danger? They can't prove she had anything to do with the medicine."

"No. And they must not." The man bowed his head. "Those soldiers out there are not after you. But they suspect her; they questioned me about a girl with yellow hair. It's getting really dangerous. They will watch her—soldiers everywhere will watch her to see if she does anything illegal." He put his hands up to his eyes. "Oh, what a life this is for you children!"

"Yes, Pastor, you're right. She should come back with us and get away from here."

A shadowy figure glided down the side aisle. Hans saw the familiar blue scarf above the red flowers.

"Hannah!" He moved toward her. "I told you to go back and wait for me in the park."

Kookie jumped up to lick his hand.

"I know. I'm sorry. I didn't know what to do." Hannah pushed back strands of hair from her flushed cheeks. "When you left, Kookie barked, and I couldn't keep him quiet. So when the soldiers came in here I followed and hid till they'd gone." She gave a little shrug, then her eyes became soft. "Oh, Pastor, I'm so glad you're all right. Thank God!" Smiling, she held out the flowers. "For your altar, it needs cheering up." He took them from her with a nod. "And what about your mother, Hans? Do you know anything?" She was serious again.

Hans nodded. "She may be in a—detention camp at—Mayerling Forest." He stopped for a second. He'd have to choose his words carefully

and not get excited. "Pastor says they'll most likely let her go—after questioning her. But, Hannah— the soldiers here have asked for a girl with yellow hair. That's you. And Pastor says you are to come back with me through to my side of the wall. He can show us a way right inside the church."

"Oh, Pastor, is it true?" Her eyes grew wide.

The Pastor nodded. "There are some loose stones in the door. But you must go now, before the guards have them sealed."

"Hans, that's wonderful!" Lips apart, Hannah stared at him, her eyes moving back and forth. "It's the only way—no need for a pass—no guards to get by—" She sounded breathless.

"Yes, Hannah. You'd just disappear and they'd never find you. You'd never have to worry again. You'd stay with us and have enough to eat and be safe."

"Safe. Yes, Hans, it means you can go now, safely." Her face looked beyond him, her eyes bright.

"Yes, I'll go but not now," Hans said. "But you must go quickly. I'll come afterward."

Her eyes lost their light. "But where are you going?"

"Oh well, I'll come soon, but first I have to go to Mayerling Forest and find the camp." He turned to the Pastor. "I can see if there are prisoners there. It will save time."

"No, Hans, you mustn't try such a thing." The Pastor was stern. "It's too risky—if there are soldiers and they catch you—it would be all the worse for your mother."

"But they won't catch me. I'll be careful and I know the way."

"No, Hans, you mustn't go—it's dangerous." Hannah's voice trembled. "Those Mayerling soldiers won't be playing ball. Tomorrow—"

"Tomorrow! Another day to wait! Look, Pastor —sir—I am not under suspicion, and I promise to be careful . . ."

Hannah's fingers clasped her cheeks.

The Pastor's gray eyes were still. With a sigh, he laid the flowers on a pew.

"And, Hannah, now please go through the wall to my house and wait for me."

"*I* go, Hans?" Hannah shook her head. "No, Hans. I never meant that I could. Even if everything was all right again, I couldn't go." Her voice was low and she looked away.

106

"But why, Hannah? I thought you said you would! When I told you about it, you seemed so happy about living with me and my mother and having all you need to eat and not worrying about being watched . . ."

She listened to him, the corners of her mouth smiling, a dreaming vagueness in her eyes. But when she slowly turned to him they were clear and sure. "I can't."

He could barely hear her words. Her fingers rested on the sleeve of his jacket.

"But, Hannah, my dear, you cannot carry medicine here to the church any more." The Pastor spoke gently. "It is not safe for you."

She nodded, clasping her hands. "I know, I know. But there is another job I can do, isn't there, Pastor?" She looked at him, lips trembling. "You can assign me to work in some other part of the city, can't you?"

The Pastor stared back at her, motionless.

Then Hannah turned to Hans. "This is my home." Her eyes were full and she spoke softly, as if to herself. "This is my home and these are my people." She turned back to the Pastor. "You know what I mean."

"Tell her, Pastor. Tell her she has to go." Hans heard his own loud voice.

The Pastor cleared his throat. "Would it not be the wisest part for you to find safety now, Hannah? Then maybe later on—"

"Please, Pastor!" She grasped his arm, closing her eyes. "There is nowhere else I'd rather . . ." She looked at Hans. "I wish I could," she whispered.

Hans' heart sank like a weight of stone. Then she wouldn't be going. The Pastor wasn't going to say any more. What else could anyone say? He swallowed hard and looked down at his shoe. Kookie was sniffing under a pew. Hans heard the Pastor talking to him but he couldn't look up.

"Son, I beg of you, return now through the wall. Time is short."

Hans shook his head at the gray stone floor. "I have to go and look for my mother." He got the words out somehow. "I have to." He looked up at Hannah. "You know I have to."

She answered with a little tilt of her chin and the quietness in her eyes.

The Pastor clasped his old hands. "My boy, then go now and return quickly to get through the wall.

108

Don't walk this street past the soldiers. Use the cemetery door. I'll leave it unlocked. And promise me something . . ." The Pastor looked at him sharply.

Hans nodded.

"Do nothing rash!"

"I promise."

"God bless you," the Pastor murmured, his hand on Hans' shoulder.

Hans turned to Hannah once more. She was looking down, her fingers twisting a button of her coat.

"Goodbye, Hannah." He made himself smile. "Later on, after—"

With a nod of her chin, she smiled. "Here"—she bent down to pick up the dog—"don't forget Kookie." She put the puppy in Hans' arms. Hans saw her eyelids tremble. Then he felt her lips brush his cheek. "Goodbye, Hans. God keep you."

He turned blindly down the aisle. At the cemetery door he looked back. They stood together, watching him. Hannah raised her hand, the fingers fluttered. The Pastor bowed his head. Hans quickly turned and went out the door.

IX

WAS it one or two hours later when Hans reached the village of Mayerling? He couldn't tell. He knew he was hungry. He felt cold in the gray air. But trying not to think about Hannah took all his energy.

Would he ever see her again? "I can't go—even if everything were all right, I couldn't go," she had told him. Would she always live over there? The Pastor had told her she couldn't carry the medicine to him any more. And then her answer: "Isn't there something else I can do?" But now, with the wall, how could anyone carry things over there?

With a glow of warmth, he thought of his mother. He must find her and take her away from

all this danger. Then everything would be all right.
Perhaps she could talk sense into Hannah. With
the wall it would be impossible for them to go on
with their work!

"Come on, Kookie," he called. The dog was
sniffing at two pedestrians. Instead of running to
him it trotted ahead through the square. Since near-
ing the village Kookie had kept running off like
this. He'd be back in a minute. Hans walked on.

Beyond the village he stopped to look around.
The Mayerling Forest towered over him to the left.
Under patches of fog the meadow rolled away in
front of him.

Far across it he saw the misty line of yellow
trees along the road. And there was the barbed
wire "wall" cutting across the far end. Through
the fog, the posts looked like a line of toothpicks.
But he knew better, remembering them last night
in the moonlight.

He found the first bush, a speck, on the meadow
where he'd caught on barbed wire. Next the thicket
hiding the soldiers and their hound. His eyes moved
to the nearer trees and the woods leading around
to the Mayerling pines beside him. Then, he saw a
watch tower! Small in the distance, it looked like

a toy house on stilts. How many more were behind those innocent trees?

He shivered, looking away. The grass bowed in the wind. There was the black river coiling toward him along the other side of the meadow. He caught sight of a rusty hulk on the bank. It looked like an old car. That's what it was! The wrecked bus the guards had found while he swam the river to safety. He stared at the road which ran beside the river and led behind him into Mayerling Village. Would he and Kookie be back here again, bringing his mother this time?

He glanced up at the pine trees shaking their boughs against the sky. Would he have the courage to go in there in this fading daylight? What would he find? And if he found his mother, what then? He had no plan. He would have to go and see.

Kookie trotted up, and they turned into the forest.

Hans would pretend that Hannah was leading him again on the path.

Specks of cold fell on his cheeks. He looked up at the rainy sky. Hands in his pockets, he walked down the road, trying to whistle.

113

Soon the pines touched branches overhead in a long tunnel. Except for the hard sound of his feet on the ground, it was silent. The trunks of the pines stood terribly still.

Hans made himself walk faster. The light was getting dimmer all the time. The pines meshed more closely together, sifting the rain.

Soon the dirt road became a wide pine-needle path, like an endless brown cushion. His one vague comfort was the familiar meadow through the trees to the right.

It was time to start being careful. If he met any soldiers, would they believe him if he said he lived in the village and was only walking his dog?

He began to walk faster. He must locate the barracks before it got dark. What would it be like? Stone buildings, guards, prison bars? If he just kept going, he would surely hear sounds long before he saw anything. The noise would tell him when to hide. With Kookie along, he could keep on—no matter how far he had to go.

Picking up the little dog, he hugged it, rubbing his cheek along the curly ears. But Kookie didn't lick his face. He only struggled out of Hans' arms, running this way and that and sniffing the air. Hans

114

stopped to listen. Were there noises in the distance? Was that a voice giving orders?

Kookie began to bark, running ahead on the road. Hans hurried after him and picked him up. "*Ssh,* boy." He squeezed the puppy against him.

Again that curt voice; muffled steps on the cold ground. Ducking behind a tree, Hans looked out to see what had made the sounds.

A long line of people moved through the misty rain across a clearing in the trees. They kept coming from a stone barracks at the side. A soldier stood by the door, calling out names as they passed. The line stopped behind a truckful of people, like the one he and Hannah had seen. They were herded together like animals, with no roof over them. Another guard stood watching them. Prisoners! Hans felt weak and gripped the branches.

Kookie, who had been twisting in his arms, suddenly sprang away. He dashed, barking, toward the officer by the truck. Astonished, Hans saw the little dog fling itself onto him. The soldier looked down in surprise and suddenly crouched.

"Oh, you're back, little one! Bad dog! Your mistress has been crying all day." Half shaking, half hugging Kookie, he called to the soldier by the barracks: "Look, that pup is back. My daughter lost him by the river . . ." He walked away from the line of prisoners, holding up the dog for the other to see.

The prisoner about to climb into the truck stopped, looking wildly about. The officer was several yards away from him, his back turned. Several heads on the truck looked around. Hans peered at their faces carefully. Through the rain, they were all a pale blur. He couldn't pick out a black shawl among all those dark clothes. What should he do now?

Suddenly two prisoners by the truck slipped from the line, running ahead into the trees.

The officer, with Kookie beside him, returned to his place. His head bobbed up, he yelled something, and unstrapping his gun, ran after the prisoners.

The other soldier left his position by the barracks and hurried down the line of prisoners. Holding his gun on them, he spoke gruffly. But several men broke line after he passed them, disappearing behind the barracks. Hearing the scuffle, the soldier turned. Then he fired a shot and ran after them.

Hans saw his chance. Taking a deep breath, he

116

dashed across the clearing, past the murmuring line of prisoners, up to the side of the truck.

"Mother," he shouted up at the blur of faces. He felt them turn, felt their eyes on him as he stared at each one. Then there was a voice, some motion. People pulled aside to let someone up to the rail.

"Hans!" The black shawl fell off her gray head as his mother leaned down, reaching out her arms.

"Mother!" He felt her thin hands clasping his face.

"Hans, what are you doing here?" Her eyes glowed above the long cheeks flushing with color.

"I know everything, Mother—Hannah, the Pastor—and Father."

"Hans, my son—" Her voice caught. She touched his cheek. "You must go quickly."

"No, Mother, you come with me, now. You can climb down quickly, the soldiers aren't back—"

"Oh, Hans, my brave boy." Her face twisted. "How? There's no time." She managed a smile. "If I run now, the soldiers will hurt the others here." She straightened, looking over her shoulder. "They're coming!" Hans heard nothing, felt nothing but the staring faces around her vivid one.

117

"But, Mother, where are they taking you? Pastor says they would only question you—they don't have proof—"

"Yes, yes, it is only for questioning. They're taking us back for questioning. Later I can come home."

She nodded quickly. "I'll be all right."

Then he heard sounds from the forest.

"Hans, you must go," she whispered fiercely.

"But, Mother, I want to stay—"

"Go to Aunt Grace. You'll be all right." She smiled, better now.

The voice and the footsteps were nearer. Hans could not move.

His mother leaned down, kissing his forehead. "Go quickly— Your father would be proud . . ."

He stared, not moving.

"Quickly, Hans!" She pulled a ball of paper from her blouse. "Take this to Aunt Grace. It's important. Now hide."

Numbly, he shoved the paper into his pocket. The truck engine roared suddenly. The motor heaved and ground, and Hans felt as if it were inside of him. His mother's lips moved, her clasped hands pleaded with him to go. Then slowly the truck pulled away into the trees. He lost her face among the rest.

The two runaways were on the edge of the clearing, hands in the air. The soldier bawled from behind them. Jolted into action, Hans turned to run. He ran past the stiff line of prisoners. He heard the officer yell. A shot whizzed near him. He kept on running back across the clearing. From the corner of his eye, he could see that the second officer was not by the barracks.

Back among the trees, he ducked down to catch his breath. Was that rumbling the truck taking the prisoners back to town? He could hear the officer cursing, the sound of feet stumbling back into line. The minute the guard by the barracks returned, Hans knew this one would follow.

Where should he run next? They'd catch him on the road. They'd expect him to go there. What about the meadow? He crept toward it, slipping between the trees. The fog had lifted from the grass; it looked wide and bare under the drizzling rain. The maple trees across the meadow were almost hidden in fog. Would he have time to run all that way? The guards in that watchtower! Wouldn't they see him? He looked beyond the forest for the tower, but fog blurred everything.

He heard the soldier behind him yell to the other. He'd have to go. In that moment he remembered the old bus by the river. He plunged out into the wet grass running back beside the forest. Then he swerved onto the meadow for the riverbank. His lungs seemed to burn. The rain pricked his face. But he kept on running.

At last when he thought he had no more breath, he dropped into the wet reeds. On hands and knees, he crawled inside the broken door of the bus. His heavy breathing rasped inside the metal roof until he thought surely the soldier would hear it.

After a moment he peered cautiously out a window. Through the grass and drizzling rain, he saw the edge of the forest veiled by mist. As it thinned away, the soldier came out with his gun in his hand.

Hans froze as the man raised the gun to his eye and slowly sighted through it from one side of the meadow to the other. The long muzzle stopped, pointing at Hans. He held his breath.

In that agony of waiting, he remembered his promise to the Pastor. To do nothing rash! What fools grownups were! They asked for promises they would never keep themselves! Do nothing rash, when all their lives the Pastor, Hannah, his mother, lived by taking chances so that other people could be safe.

The soldier slowly lowered his gun and turned back into the trees. Hans sank down, wiping his forehead with his sleeve. Well, he was safe. The Pastor should be satisfied! After a few minutes, he could easily go back along the riverbank to the road through Mayerling Village and return to the church as he'd promised. And what then? Go back over the wall and wait?

He buried his face in the crook of his arm and lay on the ground. The tears ran down but he made no sound. And he thought of the whole long day: the wet cold night of running; the endless day of hiding and looking and hoping; the huddle of people along the barbed wire; the Pastor bowing his head; and Hannah's face in the moonlight, white and proud. My father died honorably. . . . This is my home. These are my people.

Hans thought about his father all over again. He tried to remember his face, his voice. And he felt like a little child again lying there. Only a vague memory touched him of someone near, always caring. But he felt quieter. From far away his thoughts came back to the present. Rain ticked

122

on the tin roof. His head was clear and he could think.

"You'll know what to do." His mother's voice came to him. "I'll be all right. . . . You'll know what to do."

Remembering the paper, he sat up pulling it from his pocket. He almost knew what it was before he read it: prescriptions for medicine from the pharmacy. But the page was blank! She had only given it to him to make him run and hide. What good would that list be anyway?

"Isn't there something else I can do?" He heard Hannah's trembling words. Again he saw her small face turning to the Pastor. "My work isn't finished, is it?" He felt his heart beat, feeling surged up in him. "No, Hannah, it isn't finished. I'll come again, I promise. I won't forget. I'll come again somehow."

He stared at the blank sky, the careless waving grass. Beyond those misty trees were soldiers and guns and spying and prison and hunger and killing. Why? He took a sudden angry breath. Why!

"We're all the same people. What right have they to their wall! This is our home."

He was on his knees. Now he knew what he

123

wanted to do. He must go straight home across the field if he could make it. He would save time. Time to get the medicine from Aunt Grace. She would know some of it without prescription, something small and important. Then he would go to the church on his side of the wall. One of the guards there might be friendly, perhaps they'd all be gone now that the wall was built! And if the stones were not sealed up in the church door, couldn't he slip a last envelope of pills through to the Pastor, certainly a note telling of his safety and his mother and the prison camp? He must write it carefully so no one else would understand.

And afterwards, when the wall was closed, he would find other ways to keep in touch. Couldn't he be the one to bring Hannah the vegetables? Her aunt said there'd be special permission to do that. And if not, there was the mail, for sending packages of food, maybe a box of chocolates to the Pastor.

There were things to do till his mother came home.

He looked through the window behind. The road was not many yards away. Fog still blurred the line of trees. Then he turned again to the forest: no one in sight. For the first time he missed

124

Kookie. He stared beyond the last pine tree. There was that watchtower small in the distance, but clear of fog against the sky. He found another farther on.

Crawling from the bus he slid down the bank. Behind the reeds no field glass could spot him. Crouching, he walked along slowly. He must take his time, not move too much. He crept on till finally he reached the plank bridge overhead where the road crossed the river. Slowly on his hands and knees he climbed up the bank.

Now he'd have to be careful, take one last chance. Peering at the forest and then at the towers, he rushed up over the bank toward the fog and the trees. He heard a shout from the meadow, a dog barked. Panting, he ducked behind the tree, trying to find the soldier. But the fog was like a blanket all around him. Down the road, he could make out the silhouettes of more trees and then the barrier.

Something black and small scuttled through the grass, up the bank beside him.

"Kookie!" Hans fell on his knees to hug the little dog who licked and licked his face. "Oh, Kookie," Hans sobbed.

Then grabbing him up in both arms, Hans

rushed on through the rain and swirling fog. The whiteness thinned away at the last tree. As he raced through the patch of clear air, he heard a gun crack. A shot whizzed past him. Then the fog closed in again. Breathless, he fell onto a coil of wire across the road.

What was this? It was too high to climb. He put Kookie down. With trembling hands, he tried to find a place to spread it open. The tight wire nipped his fingers. His head was throbbing. At last he found a break at one end. With one foot and both hands, he made a gap and stumbled through with Kookie behind him.

Gasping, he clutched a post of the barrier. On his stomach Kookie began squeezing his head and then his body under the lowest wire which Hans held up for him. Trembling so he could hardly stand, Hans climbed on a wire and swung one leg and then the other over the top. The barbs scraped down his bare legs, but he felt nothing until his feet touched solid ground.

He was back over the wall.